A Shock for Mini

Karen Ball ● **Jon Stuart**

Contents

Welcome to Micro World!   page 2

Our Adventures So Far   page 6

One Step Closer   page 15

OXFORD

UNIVERSITY PRESS

Macro Marvel
(billionaire inventor)

Welcome to Micro World!

Macro Marvel invented Micro World – a micro-sized theme park where you have to shrink to get in.

A computer called **CODE** controls Micro World and all the robots inside – MITEs and BITEs.

A MITE

A BITE

Disaster strikes!

CODE goes wrong on opening day.
CODE wants to shrink the world.

Macro Marvel is trapped inside the park ...

Enter Team X!

Four micro agents – *Max, Cat, Ant* and *Tiger* – are sent to rescue Macro Marvel and defeat CODE.

Mini Marvel joins Team X.

Mini Marvel
(Macro's daughter)

Together they have to:

- Defeat the BITEs
- Collect the CODE keys
- Rescue Macro Marvel
- Stop CODE
- Save the world!

CODE key
(12 collected)

Look at the map on page 4. You are in the Marvel Towers zone.

3

Before you read

Word alert

- Which is the tricky part in each of these words?

  could   would

- Which letters make the long /oo/ sound in these words?

  soon   room   chewed

- Look out for other words that include the long /oo/ sound when you are reading.

What does it mean?

fizzing – bubbling

Into the zone

- Why is Mini determined to get into Marvel Towers?
- Can you remember what happened to Macro Marvel on the opening day?

5

Our Adventures So Far

Team X, Mini and Rex were outside Marvel Towers. Everyone was sleeping but Mini and Rex couldn't sleep. To fill the time, Mini decided to make notes about their adventures.

My Micro World Adventures

×

My stomach is fizzing with nerves.
Soon, I hope we can rescue the brilliant
inventor Macro Marvel. Or as I call
him, my dad!

Dad has not been seen since he went through the Shrinker into Micro World. He has been captured by CODE. We have now reached Marvel Towers. CODE is here!

I couldn't have got this far without Team X. Max, Cat, Ant and Tiger have been fantastic. Rex has helped too, of course!

We've been through twelve zones and have tracked down all the BITEs. Some were rather scary! At times I thought we wouldn't be able to defeat them! We managed though, so now we have twelve CODE keys.

When I look up, I can see the giant eye of CODE. It gives me the creeps. I think Dad could be in the room at the top of Marvel Towers.

Mini put down her Gizmo and chewed her lip nervously.

"How can I sleep at a time like this? My dad could be up there right now!" she whispered.

"Snorp," said Rex.

Mini sighed. She hoped she would have some good news soon.

Now you have read ...
Our Adventures So Far

Shrink the story

What were the most important events in Mini's Micro World Adventures? What would you add to Mini's notes?

Think about the story

How was Mini feeling when she was making notes?

🔍 Look for evidence in the story.

Here are some clues to help you:

- **Page 7**: Mini tells us how her stomach is feeling.
- **Page 11**: Mini tells us how the giant eye of CODE makes her feel.
- **Page 12**: Mini talks about why she is wide awake.

What next?

What do you think Mini will do next?

- Go to sleep.
- Look for her dad.
- Make more notes.

Before you read

Word alert

- Look at the words. Here are the sounds to remember when you are reading this story:

  should   stool   blue
  intrude   flew   control

- Look out for more words with these sounds when you are reading.

What does it mean?

nano – something so small it can only be seen with a microscope

Into the zone

- What do you think has happened to Macro Marvel?
- Do you think it will be easy to rescue Macro Marvel?

14

One Step Closer

Chapter 1 – The Giant Sneeze

Suddenly, Mini heard a giant sneeze and looked up.

"That's my dad!" she whispered to Rex. "No one can sneeze louder than him!"

"Snorp," Rex replied.

Max, Cat, Ant and Tiger were fast asleep. Tiger was snoring loudly.

"I can't wait any longer. I have to rescue Dad," she said. "Let's go, Rex. There's no time to waste!"

Marvel Towers looked like a huge letter M. On top of it was the eye of CODE. It was bright red and it scared Mini. She hoped it couldn't see her.

Mini ran up the stairs two at a time and
Rex flew after her. It was a long way up.
At the top Mini stopped to catch her breath.
It was then she noticed that the door to
the Control Room was already open.

Mini stepped inside. There was an eerie glow coming from the large screens. Someone was sitting in a big leather chair, briskly pressing the controls on the desk.

"Welcome, Mini," said a cold voice.
The leather chair slowly swivelled round.
Mini staggered back.
"Dad!" she cried.

Macro Marvel's eyes burned bright red. He looked like her dad, but something was wrong. His nose was running, and he was shivering. He blew his nose hard. He looked like he had a cold.

"Come here," Marvel ordered rudely.

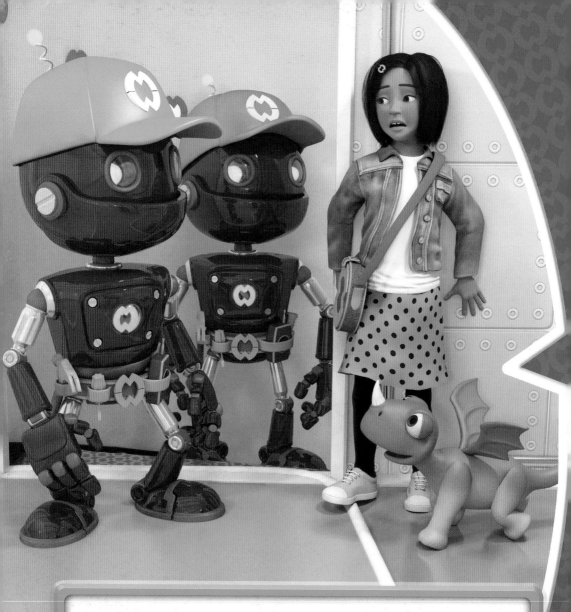

Mini didn't move. She heard the pounding
of metal feet on the stairs. She looked
round and saw two MITE guards in the
doorway. She was trapped!

Chapter 2 – Missing Mini

Ant sat up and rubbed his eyes. Max, Cat and Tiger were still asleep, but where were Mini and Rex?

Ant shook Tiger awake.

"Tiger, wake up! Mini's gone! Rex has gone too!"

Tiger leapt up.

"They must be up there!" he said, pointing towards the open door of Marvel Towers. They quickly woke Max and Cat.

"We should go after them!" Max said.
"They could be in danger."
As they picked up their backpacks, Ant paused.
"We shouldn't just rush in, we don't know what's ahead," he said.
"That's true," replied Max. "CODE could be very powerful now. Follow me but be very quiet."

Max led the way up the winding staircase. He held a finger to his lips, warning the others that they should stay quiet and not intrude. He peered around the door. A man in a blue suit was sitting in a big leather chair. He didn't look well and his eyes were burning red.

"That's Macro Marvel!" Cat whispered. "I've seen pictures of him on Mini's Gizmo." Near Marvel, Mini was sitting hunched on a stool. Rex was sitting at her feet. Mini's Gizmo was on the desk beside Marvel.

"Look at Macro Marvel's eyes," said Tiger. "He's got red eyes like a BITE ready to attack!"

"I wonder ..." said Ant thoughtfully, as he put on his X-ray glasses.

Ant stared at Marvel. Then he let out a small cry of surprise and clamped his hand over his mouth.

"There's a BITE inside him!" gasped Ant.

"If there's another BITE, there must be another CODE key," said Cat.

"The BITE must be controlling Macro Marvel," Max whispered. "We must get the BITE and free him. Then he can help us stop CODE. The future of the world could depend on it."

"How can we get the BITE?" Tiger asked.
"We'll need to get inside Macro Marvel,"
Ant replied.
"That's impossible!" said Cat.

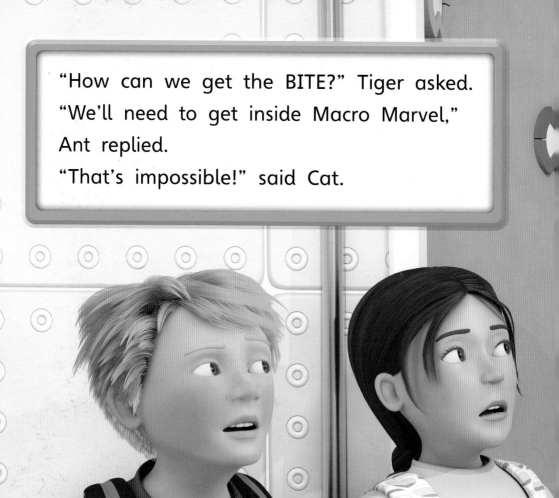

"No, it's not. All we need to do is shrink to micro-size, then shrink again ... to nano-size," said Max. "Then we could use Hawkwing to go in through Macro Marvel's mouth."
The four friends looked at each other. They'd never been inside a human before!

Now you have read ...
One Step Closer

Shrink the story

What were the most important events in this story?
Think of one sentence to summarise each chapter.

Take the temperature

How do Mini's feelings change during the story?
How frightened is Mini in each picture?
Give a rating using the 0–5 scale.

Page 15:
Mini hears
a sneeze.

Page 20: Mini
sees her dad
for the first time.

Page 22: Mini
is trapped.

Reading speech

Read pages 27–31 again. Can you change your
voice to sound like each character?